Pinocchio

Written by Lorraine Horsley
Illustrated by Monica Carretero

This is the story of a piece of wood,
and how the piece of wood was
turned into a real little boy.

7

A man called Geppetto made a puppet out of the piece of wood.

As soon as Geppetto had made the puppet, it began to talk. Then it began to walk!

"You can walk and talk just like a real little boy!" said Geppetto. He called the puppet Pinocchio.

Geppetto had always wanted a little boy of his own.

"I wish you could be a real boy, Pinocchio," he said.

Geppetto told Pinocchio
he had to go to school.
But Pinocchio was a naughty
little puppet. He did not want
to go to school, so he ran
away into the wood.

He met a fairy in the wood. The fairy said, "Geppetto told you to go to school. Did you go?"

Pinocchio told a lie. He told the fairy he had gone to school.
As soon as he told the lie, his nose got longer and longer.

15

"You naughty little puppet!" said the fairy. "If you tell lies, your nose will get longer and longer!"

Pinocchio began to cry, so the fairy made his nose little again.

"I want to be good," said Pinocchio. "Can you make me into a real little boy?"

17

"Yes," said the fairy. "I can make you into a real boy. But you must go back home and be a good boy. Good boys do as they are told. They go to school and they do not tell lies!"

"I will be a good boy," said Pinocchio, and off he went.

Pinocchio ran all the way home as fast as he could. But when he got there, Geppetto was not at home. He had gone to look for Pinocchio.

21

"I must go to look for Geppetto,"
said Pinocchio, and off he went.

He walked for days and days,
but it was no good. Geppetto
could not be found.

Then Pinocchio met some naughty
boys. They took him to Toyland,
where they played and played
all day long.

Then one day, all the naughty boys in Toyland began to turn into donkeys. Pinocchio turned into a donkey, too!

Pinocchio ran away. He ran for days and days. At last, he got to the sea and jumped in the water.

As soon as he was in the water, Pinocchio turned into a puppet again.

But there was a huge fish in the sea. Pinocchio could not get away and the fish swallowed him in just one bite!

31

Pinocchio found Geppetto inside the fish, too. The fish had swallowed him when Geppetto was looking for Pinocchio.

Pinocchio was so happy he had found Geppetto at last.

"I will save you," Pinocchio told Geppetto. "I will get you out of here."

33

Pinocchio made a huge fire out of all the pieces of wood he found in the fish.

The fire made the fish sneeze and sneeze and sneeze...

At last, the fish sneezed Geppetto and Pinocchio back out into the sea. Pinocchio pulled Geppetto out of the water and took him all the way home.

Pinocchio got Geppetto into bed and took care of him. Soon, Geppetto was well again.

The next day, Pinocchio went back to school, just as the fairy had told him he must.

Then one day, the fairy came
to Geppetto's home.

"You are a good little puppet,"
she told Pinocchio. "You saved
Geppetto and took care of him.
You did as I told you and you went
to school. And so, I will turn you
into a real little boy!"

Pinocchio went to find Geppetto.

"Look at me!" he said. "I am a real boy at last!" And he began to jump for joy. Geppetto jumped for joy, too.

43

Geppetto was so happy,
he began to cry.

"At last I have my wish. I have
a little boy all of my own."

And that is the story of how
a piece of wood became a
real little boy.

45

How much do you remember about the story of Pinocchio? Answer these questions and find out!

- What happens when Pinocchio tells a lie?

- What do all the naughty boys turn into?

- What swallows Pinocchio?

- Who does Pinocchio meet inside the big fish?

- How do Pinocchio and Geppetto escape from the fish?

- What does the fairy turn Pinocchio into?

Unjumble these words to make words from the story, then match them to the correct pictures.

Ponichoci   **ishf**   **Geetoppt**

Pinocchio   fish   Gppetto

yifar   **ondkey**

fairy   donkey

Tick the books you've read!

Level 3

Puss in Boots ☐	Angry Birds: Matilda Saves the Day ☐	Sharks ☐	Thumbelina ☐	Aladdin ☐	You won't like this present as much as I DO! ☐	The Elves and the Shoemaker ☐
Jack and the Beanstalk ☐	Furi on Music Island ☐	Poppet Stows Away ☐	Rapunzel ☐	The Red Knight ☐	The Jungle Book ☐	Roxy and the Great Escape ☐
Hansel and Gretel ☐	Harry and the Bucketful of Dinosaurs ☐	Angry Birds: Bomb's Best Birthday ☐	Angry Birds: Cheerful Chuck! ☐			

Level 4

Dick Whittington ☐	Knights and Castles ☐	Peter and the Wolf ☐	Pinocchio ☐	I am Inventing an Invention ☐	Harry and the Dinosaurs United ☐	Heidi ☐
Katsuma and the Art Thief ☐	Luvli and the Glump-a-tron ☐	The Pied Piper of Hamelin ☐	Sam and the Robots ☐	Snow White and the Seven Dwarfs ☐	The Wizard of Oz ☐	The Little Mermaid ☐
Alice in Wonderland ☐	Oddie The Hero ☐	Angry Birds: Red and the Great Fling-off ☐	Angry Birds: Stella ☐